Something QUEER is going on

(a mystery)

by
Elizabeth Levy

illustrated
by
Mordicai Gerstein

A Young Yearling Book

Published by
Dell Publishing
a division of
The Bantam Doubleday Dell Publishing Group, Inc.
666 Fifth Avenue
New York, New York 10103

To each other

The trademark Yearling® is registered in the U.S. Patent
and Trademark Office.

ISBN: 0-440-47974-6

**Reprinted by arrangement with Delacorte Press
Printed in the United States of America** ·

July 1982

10 9 8 7

CW

One day Jill came home and Fletcher wasn't there.

Jill asked Linda, the woman who took care of her during the day, "Have you seen Fletcher?"

LINDA

"He was sitting out there on the front steps around lunchtime," said Linda.

"You haven't seen him since?" asked Jill.

"I haven't looked for him," said Linda.

Jill went outside to look around. She ran into her friend Gwen. "Hey," she said, "I can't find Fletcher!"

"What do you mean?" asked Gwen. "Your dog never needs finding. He never goes anywhere."

"That's just the point," said Jill. "He wasn't in front of the house when I got home."

Fletcher was not the kind of dog to run away.
In fact, Fletcher hardly ever moved at all.

FLETCHER
LYING ON THE
FRONT STEPS

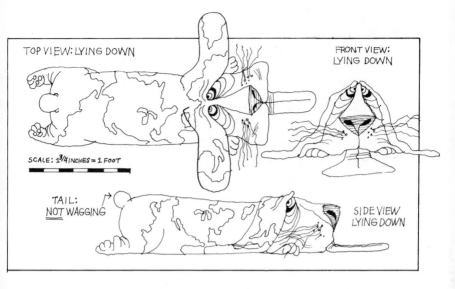

TOP VIEW: LYING DOWN

FRONT VIEW: LYING DOWN

SCALE: 1³/₄ INCHES = 1 FOOT

TAIL: NOT WAGGING

SIDE VIEW: LYING DOWN

Every day when Jill came home, Fletcher got up off the front steps and wagged his tail. This was exercise to Fletcher.

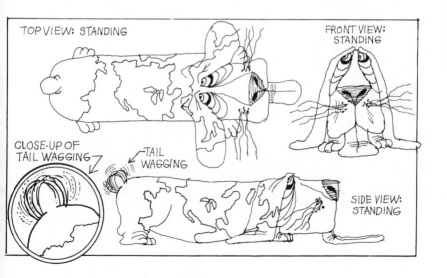

TOP VIEW: STANDING

FRONT VIEW: STANDING

CLOSE-UP OF TAIL WAGGING

TAIL WAGGING

SIDE VIEW: STANDING

"Maybe something queer is going on," said Gwen. "Do you think somebody snatched Fletcher?" She began to tap the braces on her teeth.

"Don't be silly," said Jill. "What would somebody want Fletcher for?"

"I don't know, but it seems weird to me."

"Look, I know you love mysteries, but that doesn't help me find Fletcher."

"We'll get to the bottom of this...I'll help you," said Gwen.

"STOP TAPPING AND DO SOMETHING!" shouted Jill.

All afternoon Gwen and Jill searched for Fletcher.

By nighttime Jill was really worried. When her mother came home from work, Jill told her that Fletcher was missing.

Suddenly Jill started to cry.

"It'll be all right," said her mother. "A dog like Fletcher can't go far. I'll call the police."

JILL STARTING TO CRY ⟶

The police said that nobody had called in about a
funny-looking dog with a big stomach.

Math

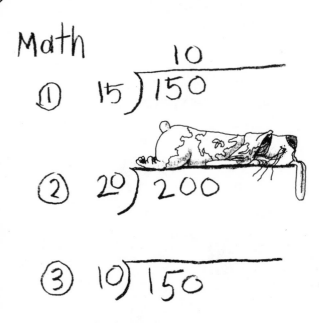

① $15\overline{)150}$ with quotient 10

② $20\overline{)200}$

③ $10\overline{)150}$

At school the next day Gwen asked Jill if there was any news.

"He's been gone all night," said Jill. "He never came home."

During math class Jill got the feeling that Fletcher was home safe. She was sure of it.

As soon as school was over Jill and Gwen ran to Jill's house.

Fletcher wasn't there.

"The police are not going to find Fletcher," said Gwen. "They don't even know him. We have to make a house-to-house search and ask if anybody has seen him."

"Not everybody knows what Fletcher looks like," said Jill.

"You're right!" said Gwen. "Get some paper and crayons."

Jill and Gwen each made drawings of Fletcher.

Then they were ready to begin the search.

The first house they came to was the Hollanders'.

"It's an awfully cute little drawing," said Mr. Hollander. "Which of you girls did it?"

"I did," said Jill. "But have you seen Fletcher?"

"How long has he been missing?" asked Mr. Hollander.

"Since yesterday," said Gwen.

"Well, don't worry. My dog goes away for days. But he comes back."

MR. HOLLANDER

As soon as he closed the door Gwen said, "Why was he in such a hurry to tell us that his dog runs away all the time?"

"Because he does," said Jill. "He's that huge German shepherd."

"I think that man's hiding something," said Gwen.

POKE!
POKE!
POKE!
POKE!

MRS. DUGA

COOKIES

At the next house they showed Mrs. Duga the picture. "How pretty!!"

"Thank you," said Jill. "Have you seen him by any chance?"

"Now, let's see," said Mrs. Duga. "I saw him a few days ago sitting on your front steps."

"But have you seen him since yesterday?" asked Gwen.

"I don't think so," said Mrs. Duga. "Would you girls like a cookie?"

As they walked away Gwen couldn't play with her braces because she was eating. But she said, "Mrs. Duga went out of her way to tell us she saw Fletcher a couple of days ago—WHY?"

"Oh, stop talking with your mouth full," said Jill, talking with her mouth full.

It went on that way all day. Everyplace they went Gwen found something that seemed not quite right. The one thing Gwen could not find was Fletcher.

Late in the afternoon, they came to a big house that belonged to Fiedler Fernbach. Mr. Fernbach was the most famous person in the neighborhood.

He made television commercials.

(ONE OF ← FERNBACH'S COMMERCIALS)

FIEDLER F. FERNBACH

FIEDLER F. FERNBACH

Mr. Fernbach himself opened
the door. "Hi, there," he said.
"What can I do for you nice
little girls?"

"My name is Jill and this is
Gwen," said Jill. "My dog
is lost and we're asking
everybody if they've seen
him."

"NOPE!" said Mr. Fernbach.
"Never saw him in my life!"

He
started
to close
the
door...

FERNBACH HARDLY LOOKING AT THE PICTURE

FOOT IN THE DOOR

"But Mr. Fernbach," said Gwen, sticking her foot in the door, "you don't even know what he looks like."

"Well...er...heh, heh..." said Mr. Fernbach, turning pink.

"Here's a picture," said Jill.

"Oh," said Mr. Fernbach, hardly looking at the picture. "Just as I thought, I haven't seen him."

He shut the door with a BANG!

"No, I'm not! I finger Fiedler
Fernbach for filching Fletcher,"
yelled Gwen, running up the hill.

"Bet you can't say that again,"
said Jill, catching up to her.

I
FINGER
FIEDLER
FERNBACH
FOR
FILCHING
FLETCHER!

(FASTER)

FIEDLER
FERNBACH
FILCHED
FLETCHER!

**FIEDLER
FERNBACH
FILCHED
FLETCHER!**

"HEY!" yelled Gwen. "You know what?"
"What?" asked Jill, puffing.

SCREEEEEEEE!

"Fernbach did do something weird. He said he'd never seen Fletcher *before* he looked at our picture."

"So?" panted Jill.

"How could he say he'd never seen Fletcher if he didn't know what Fletcher looked like?"

Jill stared at Gwen. "You know," she said. "You really *have* something!"

"See!" said Gwen. "SOMETHING QUEER IS GOING ON!"

"Fernbach could only know what Fletcher looks like if he *has* Fletcher," said Jill. "But what would Fernbach want Fletcher for?"

"That's what we've got to find out," said Gwen. "We've got to go back and watch his every move!"

"It's getting dark," said Jill. "My mother will be worried."

"Well, all right, let's meet in the morning and follow him."

"How?" asked Jill. "He'll go to work in his car. Besides, we've got to go to school."

Gwen played with her braces. It was a problem. Finally she said, "Your mother's okay...isn't she?"

"Yeah, she's okay," said Jill.

"Well, we need her," said Gwen.

Gwen and Jill told Jill's mother everything.

"Let me get this straight," said Jill's mother. "Fernbach said he had never seen Fletcher before he even looked at the drawing, and Fernbach slammed the door on you?"

Gwen and Jill nodded their heads.

"Now, you want me to skip work tomorrow and follow Fernbach?" asked Jill's mother.

"We want to go with you," said Jill. "You also have to write a note to get us out of school."

"Well," said Jill's mother, "I don't know what I'll tell my boss, and I'll look silly if Fernbach catches me— but I'll do it."

The next morning, they got up very early. They drove to Fernbach's house and sat where they were hidden by a big tree.

"Well, here we are," said Jill's mother.

Jill didn't know why, but she wished she had gone to school and never mentioned Fernbach to her mother.

Gwen was too excited to talk.

The garage door went up.

(THIS IS WHAT JILL'S MOTHER SAW IN HER REARVIEW MIRROR)

Jill's mother started her car as quietly as she could. When Fernbach moved...she was ready.

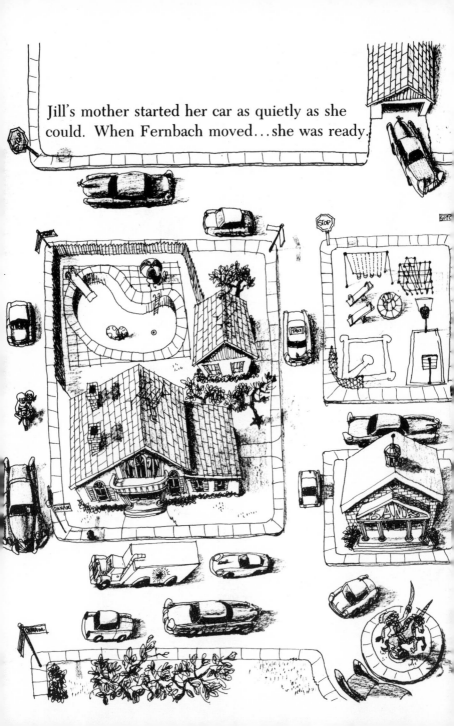

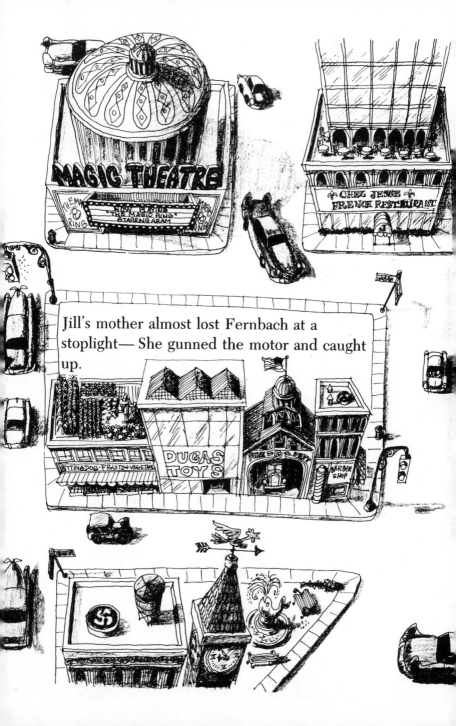

Jill's mother almost lost Fernbach at a stoplight— She gunned the motor and caught up.

Fernbach stopped in front of a big building.

"He's just going to work," said Jill. "The whole thing's a joke."

"Come on," said Jill's mother. "We're going to get to the bottom of this."

A woman at the desk asked, "Can I help you?"

"These are the children for the soap commercial," said Jill's mother with a big smile.

"Go right in," said the woman, pointing to a big door marked PRIVATE.

"Mother," said Jill, "you're going to get us in trouble."

"Shhh," said Jill's mother.

Just then, they saw Fernbach go through a door at the end of the hall. (Luckily—Fernbach did not see them.)

"Let's go," whispered Gwen.

"Do you think Fletcher's in there?" whispered Jill's mother.

"I thought you were the one who was sure," Jill whispered back.

"We're going in there," said Gwen. "It's now or NEVER!"

DO NOT ENTER

It was a big room, full of movie equipment and
bright lights.

FLETCHER!

In the middle, with a big can of dog food by his side, lay Fletcher. "HOW DARE YOU COME IN IN THE MIDDLE OF SHOOTING!" shouted Fernbach.

Jill ran to Fletcher, who got up and wagged his tail.

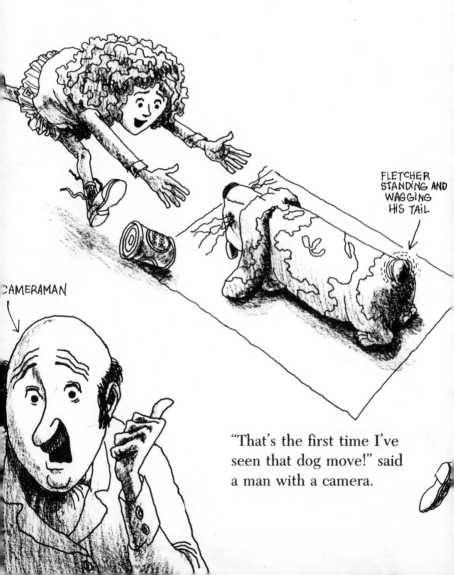

FLETCHER STANDING AND WAGGING HIS TAIL

CAMERAMAN

"That's the first time I've seen that dog move!" said a man with a camera.

"YOU STOLE JILL'S DOG!" yelled Gwen, pointing at Fernbach.

Fernbach got red in the face. "I just borrowed him."

"You can't borrow a dog without asking," said Jill.

"I saw him on the street," Fernbach stuttered. "He got up and followed me, and I didn't know whose dog he was."

"You're a liar!" said Gwen.

"Yeah," said Jill. "You're a big liar. Fletcher didn't follow you 'cause he never follows anyone. You'd be the last person he'd follow."

TAP
TAP
TAP

THE MAN WHO
PUTS UP THE
LIGHTS ↓

"Mr. Fernbach," said Jill's mother, "I don't think you're telling the truth. Jill and Gwen are right. You took Fletcher, and I want to know why."

"I'll tell you why," said the man with the camera. "Your dog is a natural for TV. I've never seen a dog lie so still. Besides, he's got a nice smile. Fernbach would have had to pay you a lot of money to use your dog. That's why he took him."

"That's right, lady," said another man. "Boy, oh, boy... stingy Fernbach."

Fiedler Fernbach looked as if he wanted to cry.

"You're a dog napper!" said Gwen.

"Please don't call the police," Fernbach whined. "I'll pay you the money. Your dog is really perfect for this commercial. He'll be famous."

(FERNBACH LOOKING AS IF HE'S GOING TO CRY)

Gwen and Jill and her mother went into a corner.

"I think Fernbach's going to cry," said Jill, looking over her shoulder.

"I don't know whether we can prove that Fletcher didn't follow him," said Jill's mother. "I'm not sure the police can do anything."

"Maybe you should let Fernbach do the commercial and make him pay you," said Gwen.

"I wouldn't want to make Fletcher a star, but maybe one commercial..." said Jill's mother.

"I really don't want to see Fernbach cry," said Jill.

"Well, do we agree?" asked Jill's mother. "We'll let him do this one commercial."

"And TAKE THE MONEY!" said Gwen.

"I couldn't stand it if Mr. Fernbach started to cry in front of everybody," said Jill.

FLETCHER AS A STAR

Jill's mother told Fernbach that they had decided not to call the police.

"Oh, thank you! THANK YOU! I know you'll love the way he looks in the commercial!" said Fernbach, trembling with relief.

The day the commercial was on TV, Jill and her mother took part of the money Fletcher had earned and gave a big party.

Fletcher paid for everything. All through
the party, he lay on the front steps smiling.

Except when the commercial was on...

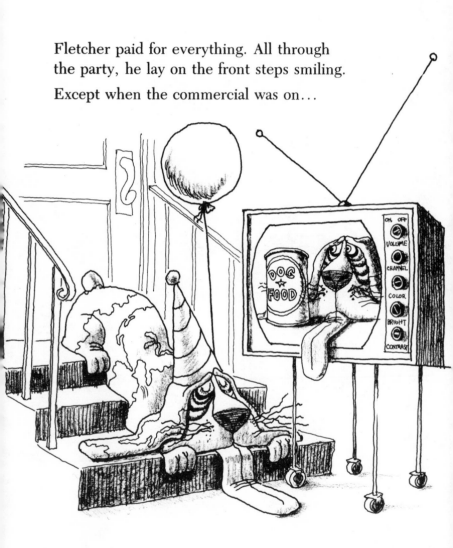

...at that moment Fletcher was asleep.